THE BAREFOOT BOOK OF JEWISH TALES

For Jon, co-creator of the three precious stories that animate our daily lives
— Shoshana Boyd Gelfand

To the memory of my mother, Jean Hall (née Iddon), who was open to spiritual wisdom from many traditions — Amanda Hall

Barefoot Books
2067 Massachusetts Ave
Cambridge, MA 02140

Story CD narrated by Debra Messing
Recording and CD production by John Marshall Media, New York City

First published in the United States of America by Barefoot Books, Inc in 2013

Graphic design by Judy Linard, London
Color separation by B & P International, Hong Kong
Printed in China on 100% acid-free paper
This book was typeset in Minion Pro 13.5 on 23 point, Celestia Antiqua, Ademo Dark and Ademo Gray
The illustrations were designed and constructed using a combination of watercolor ink,
chalk pastel, colored pencil and digital layering
Design concept and page layouts by Amanda Hall

ISBN 978-1-84686-884-9

Library of Congress Cataloging-in-Publication Data is available under
LCCN 2012043380

1 3 5 7 9 8 6 4 2

Author's Note: According to Jewish tradition, one should be very careful about writing God's four-letter Hebrew name (the tetragrammaton) because, once it is written, that page needs to be treated as holy text. But that only applies to the Hebrew, not to an English translation (though some people abbreviate it in English as well, as a sign of respect). As these are stories written in English, I have opted to write God's name in full.

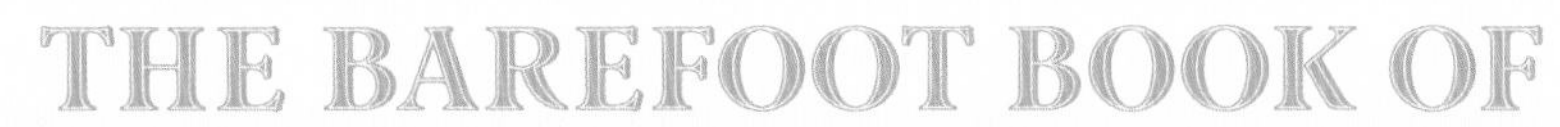

JEWISH TALES

Written by Shoshana Boyd Gelfand
Illustrated by Amanda Hall
Narrated by Debra Messing

Barefoot Books
step inside a story

CONTENTS

THE POWER OF STORY

Long ago in Poland, there lived a famous and holy rabbi, the Ba'al Shem Tov. Whenever his people were in danger, he would go to a special place he knew, deep in the forest. He would gather some twigs and branches, light a fire and say a prayer. Every time he did this, God would answer his prayer, and something would happen to save the Jewish people from the trouble they were in. The rabbi and all his people would thank God for rescuing them.

Time went by, and the Ba'al Shem Tov died, but he had a favorite student, someone who'd been by his side for many years and knew that his teacher had gone to the forest to pray for help in all those times of crisis. This student was the only person who knew exactly where his master had chosen to lay and light his fire. Called the Maggid of Mezeritch, he was now an old man himself. Now it was his turn. Whenever his people asked him to pray to God to rescue them from those who wished to hurt them, he would go to the same place in the forest to which his teacher had gone. There, he would bow his head and say, "Dear God, I do not know how to light the fire, but I know the place and I remember the prayer, so that must be enough." Then he would say the prayer, and indeed this was enough. God would hear and keep the Jewish people safe.

The years passed and the time came when the Maggid of Mezeritch died. His student, Moshe Leib of Sasov, knew exactly where to go in times of trouble, but he could not remember much else of the ritual that his teacher had performed. So whenever his community was threatened, he would go to the same place in the forest and pray. "Dear God," he would say, "I do not

know how to light the fire, and I do not know the words to the prayer, but I know this place and that must be enough." And it was. God heard his prayers and saved his people.

That generation passed away, as the years rolled by, and so it was that the rabbi from the next generation, who was called Israel of Riszhyn, had to ask God for help. By then, so much time had passed that no one remembered much of anything that the very first rabbi, the great Ba'al Shem Tov, had done. Still, Israel of Riszhyn had to try. "I do not know how to light the fire," he prayed. "I do not know the exact words to the prayer. I don't even know the place in the forest. But I can tell the story, and that must be enough." And it was.

That is the power of prayer. It is also the power of the story. Even when we can no longer remember exactly where to go or what to do or what words to say, we can tell the story and that will be enough.

This is a book of stories, to be told from one generation to the next. Tell the stories and pass them on. Whatever your child remembers, that will be enough.

ELIJAH'S WISDOM

Many years ago, there were prophets who walked the earth. The prophets were messengers of God, and their job was to make the world more just and peaceful. The prophets were special. God spoke to them directly, and they could hear and understand what the divine voice said. God asked them to tell the people what they were supposed to do. "Go and speak to the people," God said. "Tell them that the world I created for them is not yet complete. I have given human beings everything they need to be my partners in making the world a just and peaceful place to live in, but now it is up to them. They must work together to bring that ideal world into being."

The prophets traveled far and wide, trying to tell people what it was that God wanted, but no one listened to them. It was not easy to be a prophet. No matter what stories they told, no matter how loudly they spoke, no matter how important their message was, no one seemed to care.

"Who cares about fighting injustice?" one man said. "I've got enough to do keeping my family safe!"

"Why should I feed that hungry beggar? Hasn't he got friends and a family of his own? I can only just afford to feed my own children," a woman muttered to her friend.

"We're tired of being told what to do," said another person. "Why can't we just get on with our own lives?"

In the end, God gave up and stopped talking to the prophets and asking them to pass messages on to the people. Most of the prophets who had heard God's voice died, and there was no one left who listened to God or understood God's vision for the world. When the people realized there were no more prophets to guide them, they said, "Now how will we know how to create a just and peaceful world?" But there was no one to answer them. All they could do was read the words the prophets had written down, and try to learn what God wanted from them.

There was one prophet, however, who had not died. No one knew he was still alive because he had run away in despair. His name was Elijah, and he was the most passionate prophet of them all. When the people refused to listen to him, he was so sad that he could not bear to stay in the towns and cities any longer. He went off into the desert by himself.

"Please, God," said Elijah, "I don't want to live on this earth anymore. No one knows who You are, and no one cares any longer or does anything to make the world a better place. Please let me die."

But God knew that Elijah was special. Instead of letting him die, God sent a chariot of fire to take him up to Heaven, where he lives to this day. However, this did not mean that Elijah's duties had come to an end.

"Elijah," said God, "you are the only one left who understands how to make the world just and peaceful. You must visit the earth every day and reward those who are trying to make the world better. Your visits need to be a secret. No one must recognize you. That way you can find out who is good and truly deserves to be rewarded."

So, since that time, Elijah has spent each day dressed as either a beggar or an old woman. He comes down to Earth and seeks out those who are in need of help. Sometimes he comes to reward those who, even though they are poor, are willing to share what little they have with others. Sometimes he comes to punish those who are behaving unjustly. Sometimes he comes to deliver a message. You never know when he might appear, but if you see a beggar solve a problem which seemed impossible, and then vanish, you know that Elijah has been to visit. Or if an old woman gives you wise advice, listen to her carefully — she might be Elijah in disguise.

One day, a famous rabbi named Joshua prayed that he might meet Elijah. "Elijah," Rabbi Joshua prayed, "I don't understand why bad people are sometimes rewarded while good people are punished. How do you know who is actually making the world better and who is making it worse? Please come and teach me your wisdom. I beg you."

Elijah knew that Rabbi Joshua truly wanted to become wise, and his heart went out to him. He decided he would help. So he paid a visit to Rabbi Joshua.

"You may follow me on my visits around the earth," Elijah told him. "That way, you will find out the answer to your question. But there is one condition: you must not ask any questions or challenge anything I do or say. The moment you do, I'll return to Heaven, and you will be on your own again."

Rabbi Joshua agreed to this at once.

So Rabbi Joshua and Elijah the Prophet set off together. They were both dressed in rags so that no one would guess who they really were. Soon the travelers arrived at the home of an old woman who lived in a tiny one-room hut. "Come in, come in, strangers," said the woman. "You look tired from your journey. Let me get you something to drink." She went into a little lean-to shed next to the hut and took some milk from her old cow. "I'm sorry I don't have anything else to drink, but please take what milk I have, and I will make you some dinner. Then I hope you will stay the night in my humble home."

Rabbi Joshua and Elijah accepted her offer of hospitality and settled down for the night. Rabbi Joshua was certain that the next morning Elijah would reward the woman for her kindness. She had so little, and yet was willing to share it all. What a perfect example this was of how to be good and make the world better.

In the morning, Elijah said a prayer over the woman's cow. Rabbi Joshua watched in horror as the cow lay down, rested her head on the straw and died.

"What have you done?" cried Joshua. "That was her only cow, and now she will have no milk to drink. What kind of reward is that?"

Elijah simply turned to him and said, "I will only remind you once of what you promised. You said you would not question my actions or challenge me in any way."

Rabbi Joshua closed his mouth. He picked up his pack and followed Elijah in silence. The next house they came to belonged to a rich man. It had many bedrooms and a kitchen filled with food.

"What do you want?" the rich man asked crossly. "Why are you bothering me?"

"We are travelers hoping for some food and a place to spend the night," Rabbi Joshua began to say.

The rich man glared at them. "You are far too dirty to come into my house," he said. "And if I were to give you food, then pretty soon I would have to share it with every poor person who happened to stop by."

Rabbi Joshua begged him. "It's getting dark," he said, "and we have nowhere else to go."

The rich man looked them up and down. "Well, because I am so generous, I'll let you two sleep over by that broken wall in the stable," he grunted. "But you must leave at the first sign of dawn."

As the two men settled into the straw to sleep, Rabbi Joshua was sure that in the morning Elijah would punish this man for his unkindness and lack of hospitality. So he was very surprised when he woke up to find Elijah standing in front of the broken wall, praying that it repair itself! As Rabbi Joshua watched, the stones stacked themselves on top of each other until the broken wall was mended. He opened his mouth to say something, then shut it quickly again. A quick glance at Elijah's face reminded him of his promise not to ask questions, so he simply shook his head in bewilderment.

The two men traveled on. Rabbi Joshua was more confused than ever by his companion's behavior. They walked all day until they arrived in a city where they stopped for evening prayers at a beautiful synagogue. Inside the building stood candlesticks of solid gold, and finely stitched tapestries hung on the walls. Elijah and Rabbi Joshua overheard people in the congregation discussing what they would be eating when they got home after the prayers were over.

The meals they described sounded delicious — fresh fruit, vegetables and sumptuous meats. Rabbi Joshua and Elijah felt their mouths begin to water. They were sure that someone would invite them to join their evening meal. But one by one, each person left the synagogue without a backward glance.

Darkness fell, the synagogue was empty and only the warden, who had to lock the doors for the night, remained. He saw Elijah and Joshua standing on their own in the gathering gloom and reluctantly offered them some bread.

"If you've nowhere else to go," the man said grudgingly, "you can sleep on the floor in here for the night. I'll be back to open up in the morning." And, with that, Joshua and Elijah were left alone for the night.

The next morning, Rabbi Joshua was once again puzzled by Elijah's behavior. Instead of praying that the people of this beautiful synagogue be punished for not sharing their wealth with strangers, Elijah said, "May each member of this synagogue become a leader of the community." Rabbi Joshua simply did not understand Elijah's actions, but by now he knew not to question him.

After another day's travel, the two men arrived at a little wooden synagogue, huddled among the market stalls of a small town. This synagogue was different from the one in the city in every possible way. The building was humble, with a low roof, only one room and no furniture at all. But the people here were kind and welcoming.

As soon as Elijah and Rabbi Joshua entered, someone approached them and said, "You must be weary from your travels. Do you need a place for supper and to rest? You are most welcome at any of our homes. We do not have much, but we will gladly share what we do have."

Elijah and Rabbi Joshua accepted gladly. Following a simple but generous dinner, they were each given a soft bed to sleep in. "This time," thought Rabbi Joshua, "I am sure that Elijah will reward the entire community. Not only did one family offer us hospitality, but it was clear that any of the others here would have gladly done the same."

Once again, when morning arrived, Rabbi Joshua listened to Elijah's prayer but was astounded by what he heard. "For this town, dear God," said Elijah, "I ask that you make only one of them a leader."

Rabbi Joshua could not hold back any longer. "How can you say such a prayer?" he exclaimed. "This is a town of kind people. Why should only one of them be rewarded with leadership? In the other town, where

we were treated so poorly, you rewarded them all!" And now that Rabbi Joshua had started to question and complain, he found he could not stop. "Nothing you've prayed for is fair at all! Explain to me why you punished that poor old woman by killing her cow, while you rewarded that horrid rich man by fixing his wall? It's all wrong!"

Elijah listened silently to Rabbi Joshua's outburst before answering. "My dear Joshua," he said. "You have broken your promise to me, so now I will have to leave you on your own and return to Heaven. But before I go, I will explain my actions so that you can understand that things are not always as they appear.

"The old woman at the first house was meant to die on the very day that we visited her. Because of her kindness to us, I prayed that God take the cow in her place. At the second house, there was a treasure buried under that wall, which the rich man did not deserve because he was so ungenerous. When I asked God to repair the wall, I was making sure that he would never find the treasure beneath it.

"As for the two synagogues, I rewarded the good people and punished the bad ones. When I prayed for many leaders for the rich synagogue, I knew that this would lead to arguments and problems. The poor synagogue, on the other hand, will have one leader to lead them wisely and in peace."

And now, suddenly, Rabbi Joshua understood how wise Elijah's prayers and actions had been. He realized he hadn't understood who was being rewarded and who was being punished. "Now I see that justice is not so simple," he said. "The only way to make the world more just is not by judging God, but by accepting that God knows best. We must act justly ourselves and do what we know is right, leaving the rest to God. And we must trust that God will reward us for that in time."

Elijah smiled. "You would have been a good prophet, Rabbi Joshua. If only more people could understand what you have just said and work to make the world better in the way that you have suggested, perhaps God would begin speaking to human beings again. And then I could return to the earth and announce that the era of peace and justice has begun. Joshua, my son, keep working towards that. Get others to do the same, and perhaps I will see you again one day."

With that, Elijah vanished back up to Heaven. Rabbi Joshua was left to ponder over this precious bit of wisdom and to think about how he could learn from it to teach more people to make the world a better place.

THE BOY WHO PRAYED THE ALPHABET

Natan was an unusual little boy. Some children love animals. Some children love football. Some children love music. But what Natan loved was letters. Natan loved letters, and he loved Hebrew letters especially. Most children who go to Hebrew school moan about it. They complain about how difficult it is and how they'd rather be out playing with their friends. Natan went to Hebrew school to learn how to read and chant his prayers, but he was not like most children. From the moment he saw the Hebrew alphabet, he fell in love with it. Wherever he looked, he saw Hebrew letters. It was as if *they* were his friends. He liked the letters more than anything else in the world.

One evening, Natan was lying in bed waiting for his mother to come and kiss him goodnight when he looked up and saw a wiggly crack in the ceiling. "Look at that funny crack," he said to his mother. "It's a *lamed*, right there above my bed!" And he was right. The crack was indeed shaped just like the Hebrew letter *lamed*, ל, but who else would have noticed?

Another day, Natan was walking home from school with his best friend, Daniel, when he stopped right in the middle of the path and pointed to a row of streetlights leading off into the distance, "Look at that line of *vav*s standing to attention on the side of the road," he said. Daniel had to agree. They did look like the Hebrew letter *vav*, ו, but only when Natan pointed it out.

"And there's a flock of *yod*s!" Natan laughed as he pointed above him. Daniel looked up. The birds flying across the darkening sky could easily have been a group of the Hebrew letter *yod*, י.

But, even though he loved letters so much, Natan was not the star pupil in his Hebrew lessons. You see, Natan loved the letters, but he could not figure out how to arrange them into words. "The letters are so beautiful," he said. "I love them, but I just don't understand how they all fit together."

Whenever his teacher gave the class a particular prayer to learn, everyone would begin working on it. But Natan would just pick up a pair of scissors and start cutting Hebrew letters out of paper. Or else he would dip his finger into the inkwell and paint letters in his exercise book. However hard he tried, he could not fit the letters together to make words. He just could not do it.

In the end, his teacher asked his parents to come and see her. "Natan is very special," she said. "He has a beautiful and gentle soul. But he will never be able to read or write in any language. While he may be able to memorize a few simple prayers by listening carefully, he will never be able to read from the sacred Torah scroll or lead the community in the lengthy and intricate prayers of our tradition. As much as he loves the Hebrew letters, reading words is just too difficult for him. Is there some other useful skill he could learn? I don't think he will ever succeed in class."

Fortunately, Natan's family lived on a farm. There were all sorts of chores that needed to be done, and whoever took care of them did not need to be able to read or write. So Natan was given the job of looking after the family's sheep. And he loved them, too. Each day, he would take the sheep out to the pasture to graze. He loved spending his days outside on the hills and fields around his parents' farm. And while the sheep were eating their fill, Natan would stare up at the birds and the trees, imagining they were forming different Hebrew letters. Or he would draw pictures of the letters in the dirt.

The year that Natan turned thirteen, all the children who had been in his class at school began to prepare for their bar or bat mitzvahs. It was an important day for each of them. As part of the celebration, each boy or girl had to stand up on their own in the synagogue, read from the Torah and recite the Hebrew prayers in front of their friends and family. "Mazel tov!" their families would cry and congratulate their children as they showed they were capable of leading the prayers and therefore ready to join the adult community. How proud the families were of these young adults, ready to begin their own journeys and take on their own responsibilities!

But Natan had never learned the prayers, other than a few simple ones that he could memorize. He had never learned to read from the Torah. So how could he mark the moment when he would become part of the adult community?

"What will happen to Natan?" his friends asked their teacher. "Can he have a bar mitzvah if he is unable to read?"

"No," she answered sadly. "Natan will not have a bar mitzvah ceremony like you. Because he cannot read, Natan will not chant the words from the Torah or lead the congregation in prayer as you will. Although he will become an adult like you, responsible for his actions and beloved by us all, he will sadly not participate fully in the community by leading us in prayer either at a bar mitzvah or any other time in his life."

Everyone simply accepted this, until one day something happened that changed the way they thought about Natan.

It was Yom Kippur, the holiest day of the year. Natan's friends woke up early. They put on their special white robes and took their prayer shawls with them to the synagogue. They were going to spend the entire day praying and fasting, seeking forgiveness from God at this annual ceremony of atonement.

When Natan arrived at the synagogue, everyone was dressed in white and praying with all their heart. "If, on Yom Kippur, you pray from the depths of your soul, using all the gifts that God has given you," the rabbi had told them, "then you will be forgiven for anything you have done wrong in the past year." So everyone was doing their best to follow what the rabbi had taught them and to focus on their prayers.

No one noticed Natan as he came quietly into the synagogue. He sat down with his family but did not join in the prayers. He did not even have a prayer book with him, because he would not have been able to read from it. Although he wore his white robe and prayer shawl like everyone else, he sat silently, staring straight ahead. No one paid much attention to him on this holy day. They were all too busy thinking of their own souls and reading the many words of the prayers written in the prayer book.

For a while, Natan sat quietly and listened to the people praying around him. Eventually, however, he became bored. "Father . . . " he whispered, tugging gently on his father's arm.

"Hush, Natan," said his father. "Can't you see that I'm trying to pray?"

Another hour passed. "Father," Natan tried again, "what should I be doing right now? I don't know any of the special prayers for Yom Kippur." But Natan's father was focused on his own thoughts and did not want his son to distract him.

Everyone was so absorbed in their prayers that no one noticed Natan wander to the back of the synagogue. There was a small table by the door at the back, and under the table was a pile of old newsletters and a pair of scissors. No one noticed when Natan started cutting Hebrew letters out of the paper, lovingly forming each one. No one noticed as the day went on that a growing pile of letters was falling gently onto the floor around Natan's feet.

And it was a good thing no one *did* notice. If they had, of course, they would have stopped him immediately. Cutting, writing or drawing is not permitted on the holy day of Yom Kippur. Neither is eating nor drinking. All one is supposed to do is pray and ask forgiveness. But no one was paying any attention to Natan sitting quietly at the back, cutting out letters all day long.

As Yom Kippur drew to a close, the rabbi stood and said, "We are about to begin the final service of Yom Kippur, the Ne'ilah service. This is our last chance to ask forgiveness from God and from each other for anything we have done wrong. If you have neglected someone, if you have misjudged someone, if you have made a mistake,

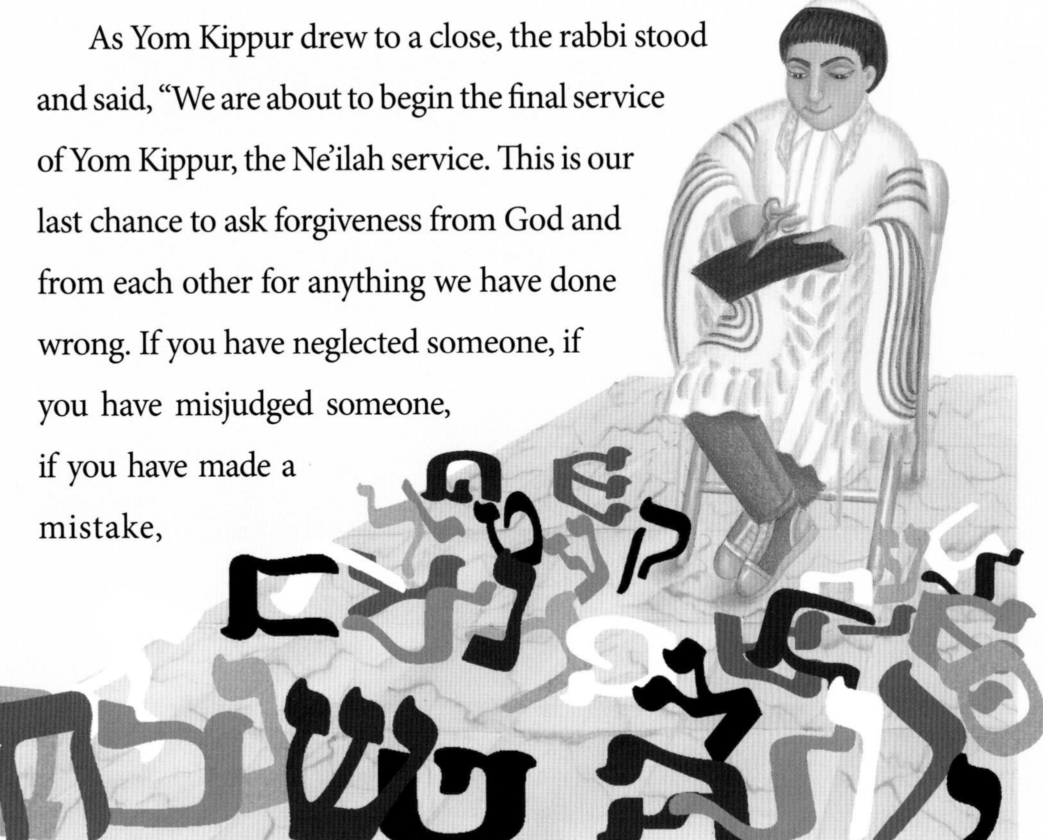

this is the time to put it right and be forgiven. Please rise for the beginning of the service."

A hush fell over the synagogue as everyone stood up for this final service, each person struggling to think of anyone they might have misjudged before it was too late to be forgiven.

And at that moment, just as everyone stood up, there came a loud clattering sound from the back of the synagogue. Everyone jumped. Natan had placed the scissors in his lap while the rabbi was speaking. Now, as he stood up, the scissors fell to the floor. Crash! All eyes turned to the back of the room. And as everyone stared at Natan, they noticed the huge mound of paper at his feet and they realized that Natan had been sitting there all day, cutting paper.

"Natan!" yelled his father. "What have you been doing? This is the holiest day of the year, and you've been cutting paper instead of praying to God for forgiveness. God save us all for this sin! I'm ashamed of you!"

Natan's mother rose to take the scissors away from him and clear away the paper at his feet. Her cheeks were burning as she strode angrily towards her son. But just as she reached the back of the synagogue, the rabbi called out to her, "Stop! Have I not taught you that all God asks of us is to pray from the depths of our soul using whatever gifts God has given us?" Then he turned to Natan, and spoke kindly. "I know that you have come to pray today too," he said. "Go on then, offer your prayer."

It was as if a weight had been lifted from the boy. With a smile, he reached down to the pile of paper at his feet and threw a handful of letters up into the air.

פתח לנו שער

What happened next was extraordinary. Natan threw the paper letters into the air but instead of falling to the ground, they simply hovered there and then began to form themselves into words. Slowly, the words formed sentences, and the sentences formed into prayers, the most soulful and inspiring prayers you could imagine.

Then, together, as if on cue, everyone in the synagogue began to read the words of Natan's prayers, reciting them as their Ne'ilah offering of forgiveness. Natan went on throwing the letters into the air, and each time the letters made words which the congregation recited together. It was as if Natan was leading everyone in prayer without uttering a word.

As the sun set, marking the end of Yom Kippur, the letters that had floated above Natan's head suddenly fluttered to the floor like confetti. The miraculous moment was over. There was a long silence. Everyone was deep in their own thoughts, waiting to see what would happen next.

Then one of the boys who had been in Natan's class at school walked over to him. "How did you do that?" he asked. "It was amazing!"

Natan looked as surprised as anyone. "I don't know," he said. "I wanted to pray and, since I couldn't read the prayers, I thought I'd offer my letters to God and see if perhaps God could arrange them for me into a proper prayer."

The rabbi came over to Natan. "My child, forgive us for misjudging you," he said. "Clearly, you understood God's will better than we did. Each of us offers to God whatever we are able to give. Your gift is a love of letters; you offered your letters and, through them, your soul. God met you halfway and put your letters into an order that the rest of us could

understand. Thank you for reminding us that any prayer that comes straight from the heart has the power to open the gates of Heaven."

Then the rabbi turned to talk to the people who were picking up their things and starting to make their way out of the synagogue. "Do you see what Natan has taught us today?" he announced. "The intention of our prayers is far more important than the precise words. Any words — or letters — that come from our hearts will reach the gates of Heaven. Let us each aspire to do that with as much sincerity as Natan, the boy who prayed the alphabet."

THE PRINCE WHO THOUGHT HE WAS A ROOSTER

Once there was a prince who thought he was a rooster. He spent his days sitting naked under a table in his room, refusing to eat anything except birdseed. The king and the queen were distraught. They were beside themselves with worry and dismay.

"What shall we do?" they kept asking each other. "Where did we go wrong? What has happened to our darling boy? He used to be a normal child, but now he won't listen to anything we say. He doesn't eat; he doesn't speak; he takes no notice of us. What can we do to help him?"

Then the queen had an idea. "I know," she said, "I'll invite his best friend over to visit."

The friend came. He poked his head under the table where the prince was hiding and called, "Hey, come on, let's go and play outside." But the prince refused to even look at him.

Then the king tried. He went to visit the prince's favorite tutor and asked him to come to the palace and try to reason with the boy. Surely this man would convince his son to come out?

The tutor listened carefully to what the king had to say. He took the prince's favorite books with him when he went to see him. "Come, let's read together," he coaxed. "I'll read you your favorite stories — you used to enjoy them so much!" But the prince ignored him completely.

By now, the king and queen were frantic. They instructed their chef to bake the prince's favorite cake. They brought it in from the kitchen, fresh from the oven and smelling of chocolate. They put it on the floor next to their son, hoping he would be tempted by the sweet smell. But the prince just ignored it, and continued to peck away at the birdseed scattered on the floor. He then turned his head to one side. "Cock-a-doodle-doo!" he cried.

"He's getting worse, not better," moaned his father sadly. "What should we do?"

The king and queen sat together for a while. They thought long and hard, and finally the queen said, "Someone must be able to help. Let us put out a declaration across the kingdom, offering a reward to anyone who can cure our son."

Many people came, doctors and wizards and magicians. All of them tried, and all of them failed. The prince thought he was a rooster, and that was that.

Then one day, a strange man arrived at the palace. He knocked at the palace gates and asked to see the king and the queen. He was tall and thin, and his clothes were old and ragged. He looked as if he had traveled a long way.

"I have heard about the prince," he said, "and I think I know what the problem is. I will need to come and stay with you for a week. I believe I can cure him but it will take time."

"Are you a doctor?" asked the king.

"A wizard?" inquired the queen.

"No," answered the stranger. "But I know what to do to help your son. My name is Ezra, and you must trust me."

The king and the queen were still worried. How could this man cure their son when so many wise and experienced doctors had failed?

"What will this stranger do to help our precious boy?" the queen asked her husband.

"I don't know," answered the king slowly. "But I think we can trust him. His name is Ezra, which means "help" in Hebrew, and he has kind eyes. He knows what he is doing, and what do we have to lose? We must let him try." So the king and queen welcomed Ezra to the palace and introduced him to the prince.

As soon as he was inside the room, Ezra took off all his clothes, crawled under the table next to the prince and began to peck at the floor. The prince was taken aback. He looked up from where he was crouching and spoke for the first time in months. "Who are you?" he asked. "And why are you here?"

Ezra was pleased. He could see that his plan was already beginning to work. "I am a rooster too," he replied.

The prince smiled at him — the first time he had done so in months — and Ezra smiled back. The two of them sat naked under the table together, pecking at the corn and shouting, "Cock-a-doodle-doo!" After three days of this, they had become great friends.

On the fourth day, Ezra crawled out from under the table and put his clothes back on. "What are you doing?" protested the prince. "You are a rooster like me, and roosters do not wear clothes. Come back here and take them off."

Ezra took no notice and just went on getting dressed. With his clothes on again, he crawled back under the table. "Even though I am a rooster," Ezra told the prince, "I prefer to wear clothes. That way, I don't feel so cold as I sit on the floor. You can do whatever you like, but as for me, this rooster is more comfortable in clothes."

The prince thought about this for a while and then, slowly and silently, he crawled out from under the table and put on his own clothes. Afterwards, the two of them continued to peck at the birdseed and lift their heads from time to time to cry out "Cock-a-doodle-doo!" The only difference was that now they were both dressed.

The next morning when they woke up, the prince began pecking away at the birdseed on the floor as he did every morning. This morning, though, Ezra crawled out from under the table and went to fetch the breakfast tray that the palace servants had left outside the door, as they did every morning, in case the prince decided to stop being a rooster. Ezra put some food on a plate and, without a word, he brought it back under the table where he began to eat it.

"What are you doing?" cried the prince. "Roosters eat birdseed, not scrambled eggs and toast. That is people food, and you are a rooster. Put it back!"

Ezra took no notice. The eggs were delicious, just as he liked them, and he was hungry after eating birdseed for four days. He went on

eating calmly, a piece of toast in one hand, a forkful of eggs in the other. The prince glared at him but Ezra just ignored him.

When he had finished, he explained, "I am a rooster, just like you. But roosters are free to eat whatever food they like. If you prefer the taste of birdseed, then by all means, continue to eat birdseed. But I like eggs and toast and all sorts of other foods. So from now on, I plan to eat whatever is on the tray outside the door."

The prince thought about what Ezra had said and then, slowly, he wandered over to the tray to see what was left. He took some eggs, a piece of toast and even poured himself a cup of coffee. He brought them back under the table and had his first normal breakfast in months. Licking his lips and enjoying the taste of the food, he looked at Ezra and smiled.

The prince and Ezra spent the rest of the day shouting "Cock-a-doodle-doo!" as usual from under the table. But whenever a meal arrived, they crawled out from under the table and shared whatever food had arrived on the tray outside the door.

The next morning, they crawled out from under the table to get their breakfast. This time, however, instead of bringing it back under the table

to eat, Ezra sat on a chair at the table. The prince watched him suspiciously. What was going on now? Then, after he had eaten, Ezra began to walk around the room instead of crouching under the table like a rooster.

"What are you doing now?" the prince asked. "How can you be a rooster if you eat your meals at the table and walk upright like a man?"

"Just because I am a rooster doesn't mean I cannot sit in a place that is comfortable to me or move around in a way that feels right," Ezra responded calmly. "I prefer to sit on a chair and to walk upright. Is there any reason why a rooster cannot do that if he prefers it?"

The prince thought for some time, giving this question his full attention. Then slowly he mumbled, "I suppose not." And he, too, sat down at the table to eat his breakfast.

That day, instead of spending his time yelling "Cock-a-doodle-doo!" Ezra turned to the prince and asked, "The Sabbath begins this evening. How do you think we should celebrate it? Even though I am a rooster, I prefer to spend my Sabbath praying to God, sharing a fine meal, studying the words of the Torah and being with my family. Would you like to join me?"

There was a long silence while the prince thought about what Ezra had said. Then, quietly, he began to cry. "It has been so long since I celebrated the Sabbath," he said. "I think I have forgotten how. And it has been so long since I was with my family, I am not sure if they will accept me back, especially seeing that I am still a rooster."

Ezra put his arms around the prince to comfort him. "Your family will welcome you back with open arms. They will accept you for who you are. And I'm sure it will take you no time at all to remember the joy of the

Sabbath and how to celebrate it. Let's ask your parents if they will join us and we can celebrate it together."

So Ezra and the prince sent an invitation to the king and the queen to come to Sabbath dinner in the prince's room. The week was over, but the king and queen were not sure what they would find when they opened the prince's door. They wondered if Ezra had succeeded in convincing the prince to come out from under the table.

The queen opened the door just a crack at first. "Oh my!" she exclaimed when she saw her son, dressed for the Sabbath and sitting at the table set with a sumptuous meal. When he saw his mother, the prince came across the room, opened the door wide, walked over to his parents and hugged them.

"This is remarkable!" the king exclaimed as he hugged his son in return. "How did you manage it?" he asked, turning to Ezra.

"Nothing has changed," answered Ezra. "Your son is your son. He always has been and always will be. He's still the same on the inside. The only thing that is different is the way he behaves. All I have taught him is that God gives human beings the ability to make choices. No matter how we feel on the inside, we can choose to behave better than we feel. The prince feels he is a rooster, but even a rooster can behave like a

human being if he so chooses. And if that is the case, then I expect that a human being can behave like an angel if only he tries."

With that, Ezra disappeared, leaving behind the reward that should have been his. The king and queen realized that he had not been an ordinary man at all, but a messenger from God.

The king thought about what Ezra had told him about behavior and choice. He realized that their visitor meant him to listen too, and to think about the choices he was making. And from then on, the king began to rule his country in a different way. Instead of insisting that his subjects come to the palace to meet him, he went out to their homes to try and understand their problems and their needs. He became known as the wisest king who ever ruled. Whenever he heard a rooster cry "Cock-a-doodle-doo!" he would raise his eyes to Heaven and give thanks for the lesson that Ezra had taught him when he spent a week with the prince who thought he was a rooster.

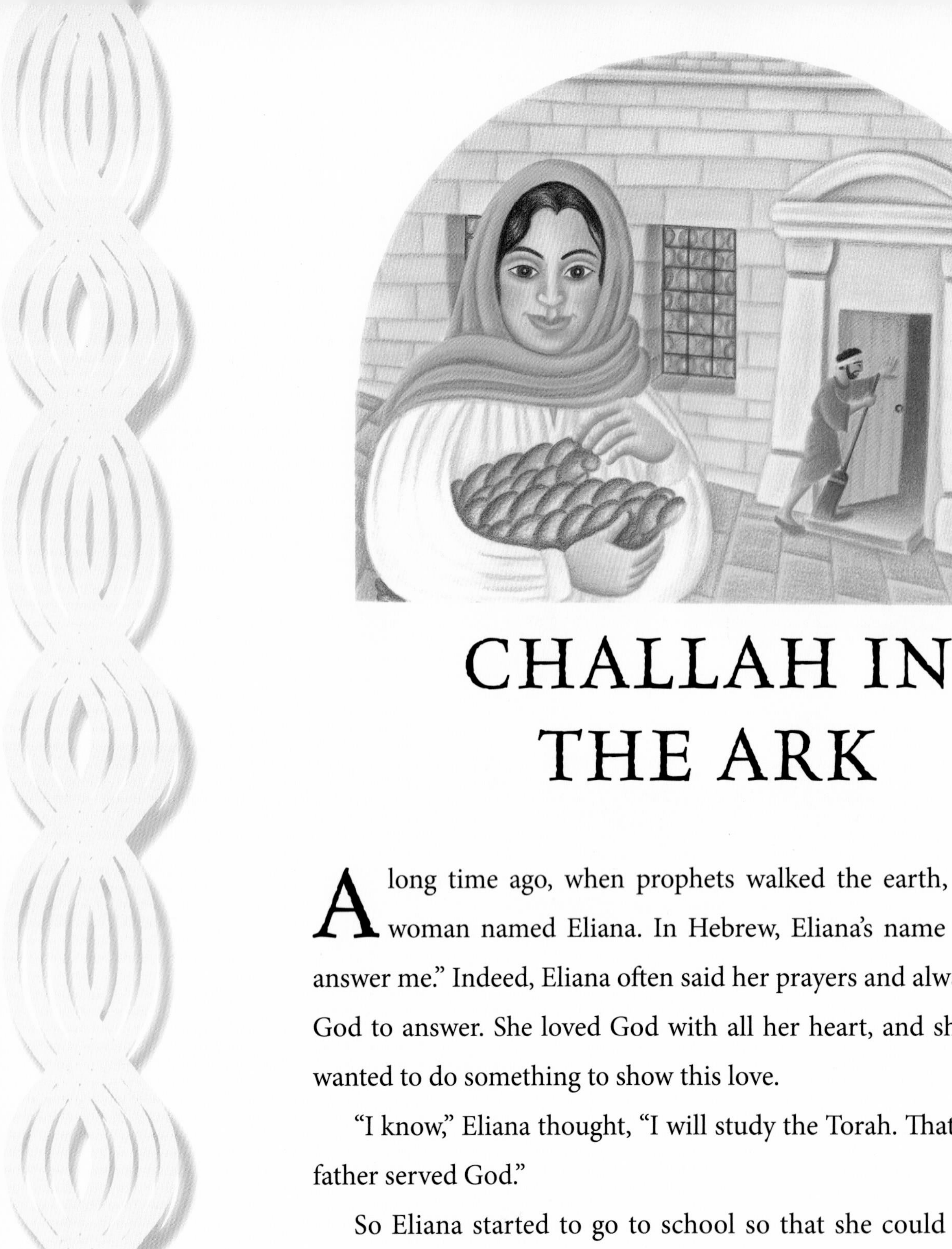

CHALLAH IN THE ARK

A long time ago, when prophets walked the earth, there lived a woman named Eliana. In Hebrew, Eliana's name means "God, answer me." Indeed, Eliana often said her prayers and always waited for God to answer. She loved God with all her heart, and she desperately wanted to do something to show this love.

"I know," Eliana thought, "I will study the Torah. That's the way my father served God."

So Eliana started to go to school so that she could learn how to read and write. But no matter how hard she studied, she simply could not manage it. Learning Hebrew was just too difficult. She was never going to be able to read the Torah herself and serve God as her father had done. However, Eliana had a big heart. She would not let herself be discouraged. She was sure she could do something.

"I could make something beautiful for the synagogue to show my love for God," she thought. Her mother had made a beautiful cover for the Torah. But Eliana did not know how to sew, and could not serve God as her mother had. Her uncle had made the stained-glass windows for the synagogue; they glowed with the colors of jewels when the sun shone through them. Eliana could not design windows to serve God as her uncle had done. And she couldn't make a carved wood pointer for the Torah as her cousin had done.

"Everyone has a gift with which they can serve God," Eliana thought. "What is mine? What can I do?" She closed her eyes and prayed, "Please, God, give me a sign. Show me what I can do to serve You."

Well, Eliana's name means "God, answer me," and God did answer her, but in a very unusual way.

The day after Eliana had prayed to God, asking how she could show her devotion, the rabbi in her synagogue gave a sermon. He described how, in ancient times, when the Temple stood in Jerusalem, the priests would bake twelve loaves of bread as an offering to God. They would place each one of the loaves on a shelf in the Temple each day.

Suddenly Eliana knew what she could do for God. "Why didn't I think of that before!" she said to herself. "I bake the best bread in town. I can bake some of my very best bread and offer it to God just like they did in the Temple. It will be *my* gift to God."

She went home and that same day, she lovingly baked two loaves of her best Sabbath bread, which Jewish people call challah.

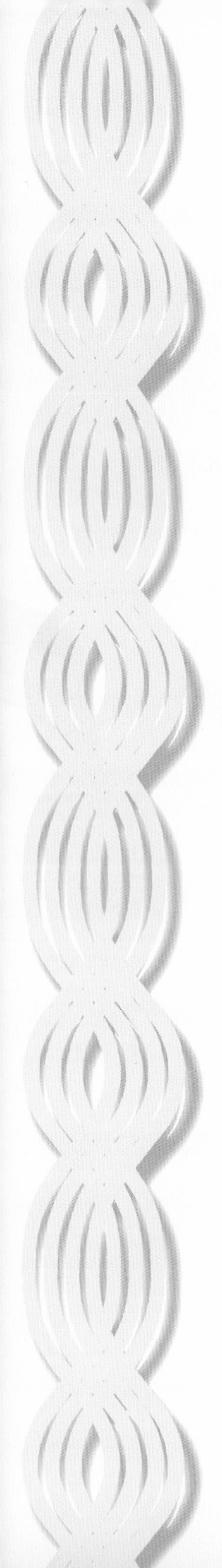

חלה בארון הקודש

Now Eliana's bread was not like ordinary challah. Most people make challah with three lengths of dough, braided together. "Perhaps three braids are good enough for most people," thought Eliana, "but this challah is for God."

Instead of just three lengths of dough, Eliana made seven strips, one for each day of the week, and she braided them together in an intricate pattern. Before separating it into strips, she added raisins to the dough to give it a special sweetness. She kneaded the dough for over an hour until it was so light and airy that it would melt in your mouth. When her challah came out of the oven, it was without question the most incredible challah that had ever been baked. It was ready to share with God.

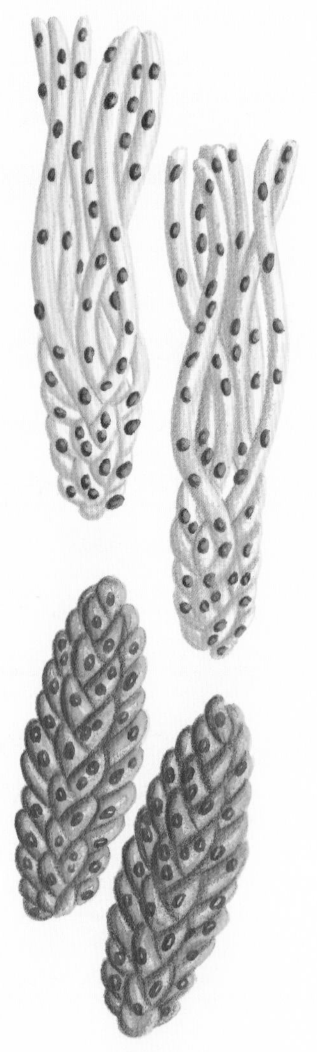

The next morning was Friday, the day before the Jewish Sabbath, and Eliana took her two incredible loaves to the synagogue. "Where should I leave my challah?" she wondered. "Where do you leave bread that has been made especially for God?"

She thought long and hard. Then she remembered the story about the priests in the ancient temple in Jerusalem, and she decided that the best place to leave her challah would be in the Holy Ark, the cabinet at the front of the synagogue where the sacred Torah scroll is kept.

When no one was looking, she opened up the doors of the Ark and placed her two beautiful loaves next to the Torah scroll. "Here is your challah for the Sabbath, God," she said. Quietly, she closed the doors of the Ark. Softly, she made her way back out through the empty synagogue. Then she skipped all the way home.

A short time later, someone else entered the synagogue. His name was Samuel, and he had come to sweep the floor so that the synagogue would be ready for the Sabbath. You see, like Eliana, Samuel was also devoted to God. Like Eliana, Samuel could not read or write or make stained-glass windows or sew or carve wood. Samuel, too, had tried to find a way to serve God. In the end, he had decided that his service to God would be to sweep the synagogue floor each Friday afternoon so that it would be clean for the Sabbath.

But this week was different. Just a few days before, Samuel had lost his job, and now he did not have enough money to buy food for his Sabbath meal. So as he swept, Samuel prayed to God in despair. "What shall I do?" he asked. "My children are hungry, and I have no money to buy them challah for the Sabbath. How can I go home without challah? Please, God, I need a miracle. I trust in You and I am going to stand here before Your Holy Ark and Your sacred Torah and wait for You to tell me what to do. Please answer me, God, I beg You."

As Samuel stood in front of the Ark, praying, he noticed that the doors were open just a crack. "That's strange," he thought. He stepped forward to close them and, as he did, he noticed something sitting next to the Torah scroll. Samuel looked around him. The synagogue was empty.

No one would see if he peeped inside. He took another step forward and opened the doors a tiny bit further. Imagine Samuel's joy when he saw that sitting in the Ark, next to the Torah scroll, were two loaves of challah.

"Praise to God!" he exclaimed. "I prayed for challah for the Sabbath, but You have given me the most exceptional challah I have ever seen. Look at these braids! Look at these raisins! Feel how light and airy this dough is! This is challah fit for a king. You have answered my prayers, God. And I thank you from the bottom of my heart."

With that, Samuel picked up the loaves and carefully wrapped them under his coat. Gratefully, he took the challah home and gave thanks to God with his wife and children.

The next morning, the Sabbath, Eliana sat in the synagogue at the prayer service, wondering whether God was pleased with the challah she had left inside the Ark the day before. Had God liked the sweet taste of the raisins? Had God enjoyed the airy lightness of her dough? Had God appreciated the seven braids, one for each day of the week?

Then she remembered that, as part of the morning prayer service, the rabbi would

soon open the Ark and take the Torah out. Eliana began to fret and worry. When the Ark was opened, her loaves would be sitting there for all to see. This made her feel uneasy.

She didn't like the idea of everyone seeing her challah. It was meant to be a private gift to God. She knew that she would feel embarrassed if everyone saw her bread.

"Please, God," she whispered, "do You think You could move the loaves over to the side a bit? Just so no one sees them and gets the wrong idea. Sorry for the trouble."

You know that Eliana's name means "God, answer me" and you will have also realized by now that, in fact, her prayer had already been answered. When the rabbi turned to open the doors of the Ark, Eliana was shocked to see that her challah had disappeared completely. "God must have eaten it!" she thought.

"Thank You, God," she almost shouted. "All I asked was for You to move the loaves aside, but You have actually taken them away. I hope my gift pleased You. You have given me such joy, and from now on, I know what to do. I will make You challah every week, and that can be my gift to You."

And so every week, Eliana made her special challah for God. And every week, as she placed her challah in the Ark, she said a special blessing and thanked God for letting her be the one who made challah for the heavenly table. And every week too, Samuel came to sweep up in the synagogue, and he would pray that God provide him with challah to feed his family. Each week, Eliana went home satisfied that she had given God delicious challah for the Sabbath; and each week, Samuel went home, grateful to God for providing his family with the most incredible challah known to man.

This went on for thirty years. Eliana grew old, but her greatest joy remained baking challah for God each week. Samuel grew old too, but he went on sweeping the synagogue floor every Friday afternoon, and collecting his challah from the Ark where it lay waiting for him.

The rabbi was growing old as well, older than either Eliana or Samuel, and as he grew old, he found it harder to sleep. Often he would get up early and wander into the synagogue. He would sit in the shadow of one of the arches and wait for the sun to rise and shine through the stained glass and make patterns on the floor. And he would think his thoughts and say his prayers as the sun rose and the day began around him. And so, early one Friday morning, the rabbi was sitting in the synagogue, in the shadow of an archway, saying his prayers and thinking of the day ahead, when he heard someone open the heavy doors.

It was still so early. "Who could be coming into the synagogue before the day has begun?" the rabbi wondered. He didn't move, but he listened. He heard someone walking purposefully up to the Ark. He looked up and

saw a woman with a scarf over her head, carrying something in her cloak. She made her way slowly to the Ark, and then, without even waiting to look around, she opened the Ark doors and slipped whatever she was carrying onto the shelf inside. Then the rabbi overheard the woman whisper, "Here You are, God. I've put a little something special into the dough this week. Enjoy Your challah and have a wonderful Sabbath."

The rabbi stood up quickly. What was going on? His chair clattered to the floor. The woman, startled, turned around to see who else was in the synagogue with her. "Stop!" the rabbi called out. "Who are you, and what are you hiding in the Ark? This is a holy place!"

Eliana was embarrassed. She stood where she was and didn't move. "Rabbi, it's me — Eliana!" she said. "Please don't be angry with me. I have nothing to hide. All I am doing is delivering my challah to God. Forgive me for disturbing your prayers."

The rabbi was puzzled. For a moment he didn't know what to say. He knew Eliana; he knew her family; he knew how good she was at baking. She sometimes even gave him some of her cakes, and they were always delicious. But what could Eliana be doing putting bread in the Ark where the holy Torah was kept? He looked at her in disbelief.

"My dear," he said as calmly as he could. "Why are you putting your challah in the Ark? You are an excellent baker, but why would God want challah? What will happen to the challah that you leave here? Surely it will go stale and moldy or the rats will eat it!"

Eliana began to feel braver. She reminded the rabbi of his very own sermon thirty years before; how he had told the story of how the priests brought challah to the Temple in ancient times. Eliana explained how

she had always wanted to serve God and that the sermon had given her the idea of offering her challah every Sabbath. And then she told the rabbi how, each week, the day after she left her challah there, the Ark was empty. "God has been eating my challah," Eliana said, "otherwise I'd see it still there each Sabbath."

By now, the rabbi was even more perplexed. "Eliana," he said gently, "you cannot really believe that it is God who is eating your challah! There must be another explanation. My good woman, I hope you haven't been feeding a thief or the rats all these years!"

Eliana felt her cheeks grow red and hot. She was embarrassed and hurt by the rabbi's words. "I prayed so long and so hard, and you will see that God *did* answer my prayers. No one knows I leave challah in the Ark and every Sabbath, the Ark is empty and my bread has gone. Who else but God could know? Who else could be helping themselves to my challah?"

"Let us wait and see," the rabbi said. He was *almost* sure that there was a sensible explanation and that God had not been eating Eliana's gift. But who else could have been taking the challah from the Ark all those years?

The rabbi decided they should both watch and see what would happen to the challah that Eliana left. He led Eliana to the back of the synagogue, and they hid among the shadows and waited. They did not have to wait very long. A few minutes later, Samuel appeared. He had his broom with him, and he swept the synagogue tiles with great love and care, polishing them until they shone. Then he bowed his head and recited his weekly prayer of thanks.

"Oh God," he murmured, "You are so good. I thank You that every week You provide me and my family with special challah for our Sabbath meal." Then Samuel left his broom by the synagogue door, walked up to the Ark and opened the doors.

At that moment, the rabbi stepped out from his hiding place, with Eliana beside him. "So there *is* a sensible explanation for what has been going on here!" he cried. "Samuel, it is not God who bakes the challah each week. How could it be? It is only Eliana!"

Up until this moment in the story, nothing special has happened; there has not been a miracle, no angels have appeared, nor any signs from God. You know the rabbi was right; Eliana had been making challah and Samuel had been eating it. There was nothing miraculous about this at all.

But this story does have a miracle. It has a small miracle, but that doesn't make it less special. For at this very moment, when the rabbi was scolding Samuel, the great Rabbi Luria wandered into the synagogue. Why did Rabbi Luria, one of the greatest rabbis who ever lived, choose that moment to enter this little synagogue? Only God knows, and that is the miracle. God must have sent Rabbi Luria to set matters straight, and this is exactly what the great man did.

Rabbi Luria watched the three of them from a distance. He saw how the rabbi was at his wits' end. And he saw how embarrassed and

ashamed Eliana and Samuel were. He heard what the rabbi said. Then he stepped forward.

"Rabbi," said Rabbi Luria, "There is indeed a sensible explanation for what has been happening here in this synagogue, and God is very pleased with the way things are. One of God's greatest joys for the past thirty years has been watching Eliana lovingly offering her challah while Samuel gratefully receives it. We humans cannot know God's way or what is pleasing to God."

Then Rabbi Luria turned to Eliana and Samuel. "You have both given God great joy," he said, "and there is no reason for that to stop now. Here is what you are to do. Eliana, you must go on making your exceptional challah each week, with the same care and love that you have for the past thirty years. But instead of placing it into the Ark, you must take it straight to Samuel's house. I can promise you that God will be just as pleased with it, because caring for other people is the best way that you can serve God. And you, Samuel, must go on enjoying your challah and giving thanks to God for it. But in addition, you should give thanks to Eliana, who has been God's messenger here on Earth."

With that, Rabbi Luria turned around and walked back out of the synagogue, disappearing as quickly as he had arrived. The miracle was over. But for the rest of their lives, Eliana baked challah for Samuel, and Samuel gave thanks to her and to God. And each week, God and the angels looked down from Heaven and smiled.

HEAVEN AND HELL

At any given time, so it is said, there are thirty-six people alive in the world who are completely good. They may be very different from one another, leading very different lives, but what they all have in common is an especially kind and generous nature. They always put other people first and never themselves. Only God knows who these people are, and whenever one of them dies, someone else is born who takes that person's place so that there are always thirty-six of these special good people alive in the world. They are called *lamed-vavnik*s — which means "the thirty-six" in Hebrew. It is said that, because of them, God lets the world go on existing. This is the story of one of those thirty-six, whose name was Ariella.

Ariella was a *lamed-vavnik* because she was very generous. She just

could not help it; she loved to give to others. Like all *lamed-vavnik*s, Ariella did not know she was special. But even when she was a child, she loved to share. Toys, treats, hair ribbons, books — she shared whatever she had. And, as she grew, so did her generosity.

Ariella's small and simple house was always full of visitors — everyone who knew her loved her and came to her when they needed help. Ariella was the person to go to if you were ever in trouble or short of something. She was always giving away her clothes or food. She even gave away the logs from the wood basket beside her fireplace. That was why her house was so simple — she gave all of her possessions away to people who needed them more than she did. Because she was so generous, she made many friends. She was a wonderful storyteller too. Children would come to her and sit at her feet as they listened, spellbound, to the tales she told.

The years passed, and Ariella grew old and frail. One evening, when it was almost her time to move on from this world, an angel appeared at her door.

"Am I dreaming?" Ariella wondered. "Who are you?" she asked.

"My name is Ely," the angel replied. "I am the angel who visits each *lamed-vavnik* at the end of their life in order to grant them a wish. Tonight, I am here to grant you a single wish before you die."

"Me? A *lamed-vavnik*? How absurd!" Ariella exclaimed.

"Ah," replied Ely. "That proves it. *Lamed-vavnik*s never know they are chosen ones. That shows you are a true *lamed-vavnik*. You have proven yourself through your generosity and your humility. Since you have given so much to so many, now it is time for me to reward you with one wish for yourself. Tell me what you wish for and it shall be granted."

Ariella thought carefully. She had never wanted riches or fame, for she knew that happiness comes from giving rather than having. For a moment, she considered wishing for peace in the world, but then she realized that people have to create this themselves, and therefore it cannot be granted as a wish. What she really wanted was to wish for things for other people, but Ely had specifically said it had to be something for herself. No matter how hard she tried, she could not think of anything to wish for. But Ely persisted and, finally, Ariella thought of something. There was one thing she had always wanted to know. Perhaps this was her chance to find out. "I'd like to see where people go after they die," she said to Ely. "Can you show me that?"

Ely was silent for a while and then he replied, "I'm afraid that request is not so simple. There are two places that people go to after this world. If you have been a cruel and selfish person during your lifetime, you go to Hell; but if you have been kind and generous, you go to Heaven. I can take you to visit both places, but don't be surprised by what you see. It may not be what you expect. Which one would you like to visit first?"

Ariella thought for a moment. "I think I'd first like to see the place you go if you are cruel and selfish."

"Very well," said Ely. "Then we will visit Hell. Close your eyes — I'll take you there." And, with that, Ely took Ariella by the hand and whisked her away to Hell.

When they arrived, Ariella thought that perhaps Ely had taken her to the wrong place. "This doesn't look like somewhere people go to be punished," she murmured. Indeed, it seemed the very opposite of what she had imagined. Before her was a magnificent palace, with ornate painted

ceilings and fine gilded furniture. There were gardens filled with fragrant lilies and roses, and trees laden with juicy apples and pears. It all looked lovely; not the sad, difficult place Ariella had thought it must be.

As they wandered through the palace, Ariella wondered aloud: "This is all so beautiful — the paintings, the furniture, the surroundings. I don't understand! What could be better than this?

But then she noticed something strange. They had arrived at the banqueting hall, which was filling with people. As the inhabitants of Hell came into the hall for their meal, Ariella saw that they looked thin and unhappy. That made no sense — on the table was the most delicious food she had ever seen: sumptuous soups fragrant with saffron and fine spices, creamy cheeses of every kind, fresh vegetables, cakes decorated with delicate frosted flowers, exotic fruits dripping with sweet juices and

loaves of bread, steaming hot from the oven. And there was so much of it. The table was groaning with mouthwatering dishes. The inhabitants of Hell all took their places at the table, but no one ate. They gazed hungrily at the food, but no one touched a thing.

"Come," said Ely. "It is time to go. You've seen Hell now."

Ariella was mystified. "Why aren't they eating anything?" she asked. "The people here are so skinny and look so hungry, but they're not even touching the food. I don't understand."

"Look carefully," said Ely, "and you will."

So Ariella looked at the table again and at last she saw why the people looked so thin and miserable. Although there were piles of delicious food on the table in front of them, there was no way for the people to eat it. Every single person had splints strapped to their arms so they could not bend their elbows, not even an inch. They could pick up the food with their forks and spoons, but, after that, there was no way of getting it to their mouths. They were left looking longingly at the feast before them, unable to taste even a mouthful.

"That's awful!" Ariella exclaimed. "These poor people can see and smell an amazing meal, but can't eat any of it. No wonder they look so unhappy!"

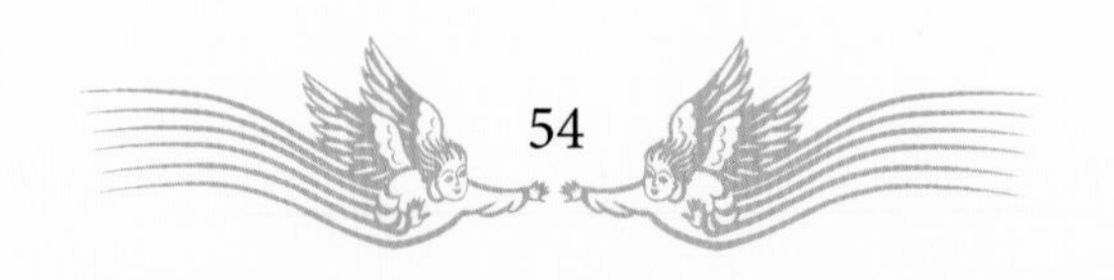

Ely looked at Ariella kindly. “Don’t forget,” he said, “these were people who never gave to others during their lifetime. They had plenty for themselves, but they chose not to share it. Here, in the afterlife, they also have plenty, but, since they refused to share with others while they were alive, they don’t know how to share now. It is a fitting punishment — one that they brought upon themselves.”

Ariella remarked sadly, “What a shame that they sit amongst plenty and yet slowly starve themselves. I’d like to leave this place, please. Can we go and see Heaven now?”

“Close your eyes and I’ll take you there,” replied Ely. Once more, he took her by the hand. This time, he whisked her to another palace, very like the one they had just left behind. It too had painted ceilings and beautifully crafted golden furniture. And it too had a banqueting table laden with all kinds of fragrant and delicious dishes. As Ariella watched, a group of people came in for their meal, just as they had done in Hell. The difference was that this group of people looked healthy and well-fed. They were happy and chatted to each other as they settled down to eat the wonderful meal laid out before them.

"This meal, eaten in these surroundings, is exactly the kind of reward I would expect God to give people who have been kind to others," said Ariella. "Here the people are happy, they can eat as much as they like, and the food is amazing!"

"Look again," Ely whispered, "and this time look very carefully. What is different about Heaven?"

Ariella looked around her at the people chatting and laughing and enjoying the feast. She saw that they too had splints on their arms and therefore could not bend them. So what was it that made these people so different from those who inhabited Hell? How could they be so happy and look so well-fed? How did they manage to enjoy themselves? She looked harder, studying the scene before her. "Same palace, same meal, same splints, same everything," she murmured to herself. "What is different?"

"Don't look at the meal," advised Ely. "That is the same — the same challenges and opportunities exist in Heaven as in Hell. Look closer — look at what the people are doing."

Ariella did as Ely said, and it was then that she saw the small but important difference between Heaven and Hell: although the people in Heaven could not bend their arms either, they were each picking up food and then stretching out to feed the person opposite. No one was going hungry. They were feeding each other — and they were having fun. When food dropped from someone's fork, or missed a person's mouth first time around, they simply laughed and tried again. It was a game. No one was angry, and everyone was getting enough to eat.

"Now I understand," Ariella said. "It was torture for the people in Hell. They sat before a wonderful feast, but they couldn't taste anything since they tried in vain to get food into their own mouths. Because they had never learned to share while they were alive, it didn't occur to them to feed the people across the table instead of themselves. They suffered in Hell because of being so selfish in life."

"Yes," said Ely. "Now you've seen the tragedy of Hell and the secret of Heaven."

"I understand," Ariella told him. "The residents of Heaven are exactly the same as those in Hell. They have the same problems and they are just as hungry. They have splints on their arms as well, and it's just as hard for them to move. The only difference is that they have spent their lives giving to other people. So when they sit down at the table, they happily start to feed the person sitting opposite them. People in Heaven don't need to bend their elbows because they know how to share God's gifts with each other."

Ely smiled. "That is why you are a *lamed-vavnik*, my dear Ariella. You understand the joy of giving and sharing. You will be happy in Heaven when your time comes. Until then, will you share this secret with others and teach them to be as generous as you have been?"

Ariella returned to her home and Ely went back to Heaven. For Ariella's last few days, she continued to be as loving and kind as ever, sharing her food, her clothing and everything she owned. But the most important thing she shared was the story of her visit to Heaven and Hell and the lesson she had learned there.

"Heaven and Hell are not just places that you go to after you die,"

she would tell the children who sat at her feet. "They're also part of how each of us looks at the world every day. People who share and reach out to others are already halfway to Heaven, whereas those who are selfish and focus only on their own needs are in a living Hell even before they die."

When Ariella's time came, she went straight to Heaven of course, because as you have already seen, she had always been generous and put others before herself. For a split second, the world only had thirty-five especially good people. Then a new *lamed-vavnik* was born to take her place. This new baby would grow up to be kind-hearted and generous, just like Ariella.

As for Ariella, even after she had died, people talked about how good she had been and how much they had loved her. They did not forget her. And that is the other thing that happens when someone is loving and giving — they are remembered by everyone who has known them. In that way, not only do they live on in Heaven, but on Earth their memory lives on too.

CLEVER RACHEL

Every child is special. Some children are beautiful, some are talented, some are strong, and some are kind. Usually, it takes a while to discover what gift God has given a child. But this story is about a girl whose special gift was clear to everyone from the day she was born. This girl was called Rachel.

Even when she was a baby, her mother noticed how clever Rachel was. One morning, she came to take the baby out of her crib, and she saw that Rachel had lined up her alphabet blocks to make the words "cat" and "dog," "box" and "bin," all standing at the end of her crib.

"What a clever little girl you are!" her mother exclaimed. She went downstairs to tell her husband, who owned the inn in their small town.

"Nonsense," Rachel's father replied. "It's just a coincidence! The blocks must have landed that way just by chance." He could scarcely believe they had given birth to such a bright child.

When Rachel started school, her teacher saw straightaway that the little girl was extraordinarily clever. She wrote in Rachel's first report card: "Rachel is by far the most intelligent child I have ever taught. I have no doubt that she will do great things in years to come."

Rachel's father read the report and turned to his wife. "I know that God has given our daughter the gift of a very fine mind," he said. "But what really matters in life is not how clever you are, but how kind. We must make sure she grows up to be kind and thoughtful too. She must always remember to help people who are in need."

Rachel's mother nodded in agreement. She and her husband were both good people, and their inn was a place of warmth and hospitality to everyone who visited it, so it was not difficult for them to show their daughter how to be kind.

As Rachel grew up, she learned to look after the strangers who stopped at the inn for the night. She learned to notice when visitors were sick or when elderly travelers were tired and needed special care. She always made sure children felt safe and had everything they wanted. Everyone who visited the inn appreciated Rachel's special gifts, and everyone who lived in the town knew they were lucky to have someone so kind and so clever living among them.

One day, a messenger from the king came to the small town, the hooves of his horse clattering over the cobbles as he passed through. Drawing to a halt, the messenger jumped from his horse and read out the king's decree. "His Royal Highness the King has decided to marry the cleverest woman in the land. Any unmarried young woman who is especially clever should make herself known to me at once," he announced.

Immediately, Rachel's parents understood why God had given Rachel such special gifts. She was to become a queen! They told the messenger that their daughter was exceptionally clever and then brought her before him.

"By order of the king, I have three questions to test how clever you are," the messenger said. "What is the fastest thing? What is the richest thing? And what is the dearest thing?"

Rachel answered in a flash: "The fastest thing is Thought, the richest thing is Earth, and the dearest thing is Love."

The messenger knew at once that he had found the right woman. He galloped straight back to the palace and cried out to the king, "I have found her! I have found her! I've found you the cleverest woman in the land!"

But the king was not so sure, even when he had heard Rachel's answers to his three questions. "I'd like to see this woman for myself," he said. "And I will give her a more difficult task so that we can find out if she is really as clever as she seems. If she is, then I will marry her without delay."

The messenger rode back to the town where Rachel lived and delivered the king's command: "His Royal Highness orders you to appear at the palace in a week's time, neither walking nor riding, neither dressed nor undressed, and bringing a gift that is not a gift."

When Rachel's parents heard this strange request, they begged her not to go. "Darling, how will you be able to answer this peculiar command?" said her mother. "And who knows what the king will do to you if you can't!" muttered her father. But Rachel just smiled and told them not to worry. She collected the few things she needed and set off for the palace.

The king was waiting. He saw Rachel in the distance and walked out to meet her. As she drew closer, he smiled. So far so good. She

was riding on a goat, with one foot dragging on the ground. "Hmmm, very clever," he thought. "Neither riding nor walking." Then he looked to see how she was dressed and saw that she was wearing no clothes but had wrapped herself in a fishnet. "I like this woman," he said to himself. "Who else could have managed to arrive both dressed and not dressed? Now let us see if she has a gift for me which is not a gift."

When Rachel arrived before the king, she looked into his eyes and saw that he was a kind man. She understood that his strange requests were because he was looking for a partner who was as clever as he was, and that he was tired of being lonely. Deciding that she wanted to marry him, she held out her gift to him, hidden inside her cupped hands. "Your Highness," she murmured, "a gift for you."

But as the king reached out to take the gift from Rachel, she opened her hands, and a dove slipped out from between them and flew into the branches of a nearby tree. The king saw that Rachel had brought him a gift, but it was one that he could not keep. As he watched the dove fly away, he smiled and held out his hand to Rachel. "Will you marry me and be my queen?" he asked.

"Yes, Your Highness, I will," Rachel replied.

The king held Rachel's hand and looked into her eyes. "There is one condition," he went on. "I know now how clever you really are, but despite that you must never question any of my judgements."

This seemed like a strange condition for marriage, but Rachel agreed and the wedding took place soon after. Rachel and the king lived together happily for quite some time. One day, however, she was out walking in the woods when she saw a poor man sitting beside the forest track, weeping. "What is the matter?" she asked.

The man knew this was the queen and grew afraid, but Rachel's kind eyes and gentle voice encouraged him to answer.

"My family has very little money," he began, "but we do have a horse, a mare. When she became pregnant, we were overjoyed. Now we might have a second horse that we could sell to buy food. But when the mare finally gave birth, she was lying underneath my neighbor's wagon, and so now the foal belongs to my neighbor. It belongs to him because it came from his wagon."

Rachel was puzzled. She frowned. "What utter nonsense," she exclaimed. "Who gave such a ridiculous ruling?"

The man lowered his eyes. "It is the king's ruling, my lady," he said. "No one can challenge it."

Rachel thought quietly for a moment. "You are correct that no one can challenge the king's laws, but that doesn't mean the king can't change his own mind. Meet me here tomorrow, listen carefully to what I tell you and do everything I say."

The next day, Rachel returned to the wood with a fishing rod. The poor

man was waiting for her. She gave him the rod and told him to go and stand by the palace and cast the line through an open window so that the hook and line went through the window into the room beyond. He must stand there, she said, and pretend to be fishing.

The poor man couldn't understand how this would change anything but he did as Rachel instructed. He stood outside the palace with his fishing rod all morning until the king looked out and saw him. It was a ridiculous sight — a man fishing, with his line hanging over the windowsill and trailing across the marble floor of the palace.

"What on earth is this?" the king demanded. "I've never seen anything so silly in all my life!"

The poor man shook in his boots at the king's anger but he answered his question. "I am waiting for fish to come from your floor," he replied. "After all, a horse was born from my neighbor's wagon, making it his not mine. If that is the case, then any fish that jump from your floor onto my rod must be mine."

The king knew at once what was going on and whose idea this must be. "Rachel!" he yelled. Only his wife could have dreamt up something like this and taught the poor man what to say.

When the queen appeared, the king took her in his arms. "You agreed when we married that you would never question my rulings," he said sadly. "Now you have broken your promise, which was the condition of our marriage. You must now leave the palace forever. But because I love you so much, I will let you take one thing with you. Choose whatever is dearest to you and go." Then the king turned his back on Rachel so that she would not see his tears. He fled to his rooms and did not come down for the rest of the day, as he could not bear to see his beloved wife go.

Rachel did not leave straightaway, however. As usual, she was thinking. As night fell and the king slipped into a deep sleep, Rachel sneaked into his bed chamber and wrapped him in a blanket. Two servants then carefully lifted their master from his bed and carried him from the room, gently setting him in a carriage next to the queen. When the king awoke the next morning, he looked up and saw the trees of the forest above him and his wife sitting next to him.

"Darling Rachel," he exclaimed, "I thought I would never see you again! But where are we, and what am I doing here? Have you disobeyed me yet again?"

Rachel looked deep into his eyes. "I did not mean to disobey you the first time, and I most certainly have not done so again. You said I could take my dearest possession with me when I left the palace, and that is exactly what I have done. You, my darling, are the thing that is most dear to me. I can live without the palace, and I can live without being queen, but I cannot live without you, so *you* are what I have chosen to take with me."

At this point, the king realized how foolish he had been. "Come home with me, my dear one," he said, "and we will live together in the palace forever."

When they arrived back at the palace, the king issued three decrees. The first was that the poor man should have his foal back. The second was to insist that the queen could and should overrule his judgements if he was ever wrong. And the third was to appoint Rachel as High Judge and Chancellor, because not only was she wise, but her kindness towards others and her understanding of the poor was the best in all the land.

THE PERFECT MISTAKE

Once there was a king whose prize possession was a very beautiful diamond. This diamond was perfect in every way. Each morning, the king would take it out of its velvet box and hold it up to the light to watch it sparkle. Because it was so flawless, if it was held in the right way, the diamond would split the light into all its different colors, throwing a perfect rainbow onto the opposite wall. And the king would say to himself, "How blessed I am to have a perfect diamond and a perfect rainbow to look at each morning." This was his greatest happiness.

There was only one thing the king loved more than the diamond, and that was his daughter, the princess. She would join him each morning to admire the diamond and the rainbow it made. The princess delighted in the many colors that shone from the diamond, making shimmering rainbow patterns on the palace walls.

"Father — look at that!" she would say. "I can see red, orange, yellow, green, blue, indigo and violet. Can you see them, too?"

"Yes, my darling," he would answer, "I can see all the colors. They are perfect, and so are you."

Then the king and the princess would carefully wrap the perfect diamond and put it away in its velvet box so that it would not be damaged. They did this each morning, and this was the highlight of their day.

One morning, the king and his daughter took out the diamond and held it to the light to create a rainbow. As usual, the princess began to name the colors. "Look, Father, I see red, orange, yellow, green, blue . . . but look, what's that? Something's happened!"

They both narrowed their eyes and peered at the diamond. The princess was right — something *was* different. Instead of a perfect rainbow shining out of a perfect diamond, there was a crack in the stone, and now the rainbow was crooked.

"Oh no!" they both cried. "What has happened to our perfect diamond that made perfect rainbows?"

They held the stone up to the light and looked at it closely. As they examined it together, they discovered a tiny hairline crack. It was almost invisible, but the king was distraught.

"What shall we do?" he cried. "My perfect diamond is ruined. It's no longer perfect! We won't be able to make rainbows anymore."

The princess tried to comfort him. "Father, you hardly notice it," she said. "And look, the rainbow is still there and still so beautiful."

The king would not listen. Nothing would comfort him. He was inconsolable. "It is no longer perfect," he wailed. He went back to his rooms and refused to come out again.

The princess was young, but she was also wise. She knew she had to find someone who could mend her father's diamond if she ever wanted him to be happy again. She asked the king's messengers to put out a royal decree across the kingdom. "Whosoever can mend the king's diamond will be rewarded beyond their wildest dreams," they announced. The decree was read out in every square in every town and village in the land.

When they heard about the reward, people came from far and wide to try and mend the crack in the diamond. First, a craftsman came to glue the crack together, but it was still visible. Next, a blacksmith came to heat the diamond to melt away the crack, but it would not disappear. Then, a master jeweler came to polish the crack away, but that did not work either. The princess began to lose hope that anyone could fix it.

And then, one cold winter morning, an old woman arrived at the palace gates. "I am told that you have a diamond in need of repair," she said to the princess. "Show it to me and I will see what I can do."

The princess found the diamond in its velvet box and, carefully lifted it. "Can you mend this crack?" she asked.

"I know much about diamonds," the woman replied, "and how they can bring color into our lives if they are held in just the right way. Perhaps I can help."

The princess was overjoyed. But then the old woman added, "I will need to take the diamond to my workshop for a whole year, and no one must follow me or watch me work."

As quickly as her hopes had risen, the princess felt them sink again.

A year was a long time. Would the old woman ever bring the diamond back? The princess began to wonder if she could trust the old woman. Why did she need to be alone with the diamond? "Why can't you work here in the royal workshop?" she asked.

"No," said the woman. "Your workshop may be large and well-equipped, but I will need to be alone in my own workshop if you want me to restore your father's diamond."

The princess had to agree to the woman's conditions.

The year passed slowly. The king and the princess missed the diamond and the joy it had brought them. They missed the mornings when they had been able to take the stone out of its box and hold it up to the light so that rainbows danced on the palace walls. But the day on which they had arranged to collect the diamond finally dawned and father and daughter set out for the village where the old woman had her workshop.

Arriving at the village, they made their way to a small cottage. It was surrounded by a lovely walled garden and climbing flowers which grew up the sides of the walls. They knocked on the door and the old woman answered at once.

"Have you fixed my diamond?" the king asked eagerly.

"Yes, I have, Your Highness," the old woman replied. "Your beautiful diamond is perfect once again."

The king was so excited, he could barely contain himself. "Let me see it! Let me see it! I cannot wait to make a perfect rainbow with it once again!"

The old woman handed him the velvet box, whispering gently, "Remember there are many paths to perfection, my king."

Carefully, the king took the diamond out of its box and held it up to view it in all its perfection. To his horror, he saw the crack was still there. Furious, he shouted, "You demon! What have you been doing this entire year? You have not fixed my diamond at all. Look, the crack is still there!"

The old woman was not embarrassed. She did not even look ashamed, but replied very calmly, "I never said I could repair the crack, Your Highness. No human being can. It is beyond our power."

The king grew even angrier. "Then what," he yelled, "just *what* have you been doing with my diamond for the past year? Why did you say you could help me if you couldn't?"

"Ah," replied the old woman, "but I *have* fixed your diamond. Look again, very carefully . . . and this time, look beyond the crack."

The king raised the diamond again. The crack was still there. He grew puzzled and then he remembered the woman's last words: "Look beyond the crack." As he stared at the diamond, he suddenly saw that the crack had turned into the most beautiful rose he had ever seen, blooming from the inside of the stone. His mouth dropped open as he realized what the old woman had done.

"You see," she explained, "no one can fix a crack in a diamond. So instead of trying, I have spent the last year carving petals onto the end of a tiny stem. There is nothing wrong with your diamond. That crack, Your Highness, is not a flaw. It is the perfect stem of a perfect rose. I could not fix the crack, but I have fixed your diamond so you can see the rose in it instead."

"I see now what you've done," said the king. "My perfect diamond is even more perfect than before. The rose you've carved inside it is exquisite."

As the king held the diamond up one more time to examine its flawed perfection, the light threw rainbow colors onto the walls of the woman's cottage.

While he admired the carving, the princess looked outside, and she noticed that there was something unusual about the walls of the garden.

As she looked, she saw for the first time that the flowers that were growing up the walls were not real flowers, but carefully painted copies. "Look, Father," she said. "These walls are just like your diamond. Each crack has petals painted onto it to make a flower. What might have been just an old, cracked wall has been transformed into a lovely garden."

"Yes, my dear," said the old woman. "That was why I needed to fix the diamond here, in my old, cracked house. Your palace is too perfect. When I'm somewhere that is perfect, how can I find the inspiration I need to make the world better? It was only in my workshop, with all its cracks, that I could work out how to fix the diamond. I practiced making the cracks in my garden wall into flowers all year. It was only last week that I felt ready to carve petals onto your precious diamond."

The king and the princess then understood that not only had the old woman mended their diamond; she had given them a whole new way of looking at the world. As they left to return home, she gave them one last bit of advice. "Each of us must look around at those things we love and accept that their flaws are what make them unique and special," she said. "It is those very flaws and cracks that can inspire us to create more beauty in the world."

The king looked at his daughter and she looked up at him. Each realized how much they loved the other, not in spite of, but because of their flaws. From that day on, they vowed to stop trying to change what cannot be changed, but rather to treasure the imperfections in the world. It was the imperfections that made each object — and indeed each human being — both unique and perfect.

SIGNS AND SYMBOLS

ARK

An ark is a place to keep precious things safe. In the story of Noah and the Flood, the people and animals were carried safely over the flood waters in Noah's ark. On their long journey to the Promised Land, the Jewish people carried their most precious possession, the Torah, their holy writings, with them in a wooden cabinet called the Ark. Nowadays, Jews use this word to refer to the place in the synagogue where they keep a copy of the original Torah scroll.

BAR MITZVAH

At the age of thirteen, a Jewish child is considered to have become an adult member of their community and may begin to take part fully in prayers and services. There is often a ceremony to mark and celebrate the first time a Jewish child leads the congregation in prayer and reads aloud from the Torah scroll. This ceremony is called a bar mitzvah for boys and a bat mitzvah for girls.

CANDLES / FIRE

Fire has long been one of the ways that Jews represent God's presence. God appeared to Moses in a burning bush. When the Jewish people left Egypt, God appeared as a pillar of fire to show them the way. In the ancient Temple in Jerusalem, a fire was kept alight at all times. To welcome the Sabbath, Jews traditionally light two candles, and each synagogue has a lamp that stays lit at all times to show that God's warmth and light are always present in our lives.

CHALLAH

As part of a Sabbath meal, Jews eat special braided bread called challah. It is a reminder of the biblical gift of manna, the bread that God provided each day for the Israelites to eat on their way to the Promised Land. It also reminds Jews of the twelve loaves of bread which were kept in the Temple in Jerusalem — one loaf for each of the twelve tribes of Israel. Challah is made of multiple pieces of dough to show the unity of people around the world and how Shabbat can help us to come together.

DOVE

In the biblical story of Noah and the Flood, when the rain finally ends, Noah sends out a dove to search for dry land. The dove finds a place where Noah and his family can be safe and at peace. In Hebrew, the word for dove is "Jonah", which is also the name of a famous prophet who was swallowed by a whale. No one knows what happened to the prophet Jonah at the end of his life, and so the dove has become not just a symbol of peace, but also a sign of riddles and uncertainty.

HEBREW LETTERS

Jewish tradition holds that God wrote every word of the Torah. Therefore, each word and even each letter is part of our connection to God.

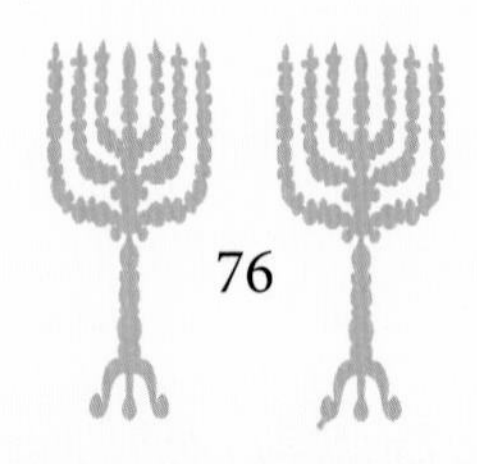

LAMED-VAVNIK

The Hebrew letter *lamed* [ל] represents the number 30, while the Hebrew letter *vav* [ו] represents the number 6. Together, *lamed* and *vav* represent the number 36 [לו]. In the Jewish tradition, it is said that at any one time, there are thirty-six people alive in the world who are completely good and on whom the rest of the world depends. (The ending "-nik" comes from the Yiddish word for "person", so a *lamed-vavnik* is literally "a person who is one of the 36".)

MAGGID

A maggid was a wandering storyteller who traveled from village to village sharing stories and tales from the Jewish tradition.

MENORAH

In the Temple in Jerusalem, a seven-branched golden candelabra called a menorah stood on the altar, and the seven lamps burned continually. Each one of the seven branches represented one of the seven days of creation, and the fire represented God's eternal presence. When the Romans conquered Jerusalem and destroyed the Temple in the year 70 CE, they stole the golden menorah and carried it back to Rome. You can still see the picture they carved of the menorah and their victory parade on the Arch of Titus in the Roman Forum.

NE'ILAH

The word "Ne'ilah" literally means "closing". It is the name given to the final service of the day on Yom Kippur. The name means two things: an ancient ritual when the gates of the Temple of Jerusalem closed at the end of each day, and the final moment of Yom Kippur when the heavenly gates of mercy close and seal everyone's fate for the year ahead.

PAPERCUTS

Because each letter is viewed as precious, many forms of Jewish artwork have developed using Hebrew letters. The art of papercutting is among these classic Jewish art traditions. The borders in this book are based on papercuts that the illustrator designed to simulate this art form.

RABBI

The Hebrew word "rabbi" literally means "my teacher." Rabbis became the leaders of the Jewish community after the Temple in Jerusalem was destroyed, and the former leaders, the priests, lost their authority. In order to become a rabbi, a person must study for many years and pass many exams. When rabbis complete their training, their teachers put their hands on the rabbis' shoulders and publicly declare that they are now leaders of the community.

RAINBOW

In the biblical story of Noah and the Flood, the flood came about because there was too much violence in the world. God wanted people to live in peace. Because there were no guns or bombs at the time, the symbol of violence was a bow and arrow. After the flood, God promised never to use violence again. God took a symbol of violence (a bow), added some beautiful colors to it, and placed it in the sky after each rainfall to remind us of that promise.

סימנים וסמלים

ROSE

In the book of the Bible known as the Song of Songs, the rose is called a "shoshana" flower. It is a symbol of love and also a popular Hebrew name (much like "Rose" in English).

SABBATH

The Sabbath, or Shabbat, is a day of rest that is celebrated from sunset on Friday evening to sunset on Saturday evening. Shabbat is welcomed with a celebratory Friday night dinner. Jewish families light two candles before they eat. They say a blessing over the wine and over the two loaves of Sabbath bread called challah.

TALLIT AND TZITZIT

During prayer, Jewish adults wear a rectangular prayer shawl called a tallit, which has a fringe called tzitzit on the corners. The tzitzit contain complex knots, which serve to remind Jews of God's commandments.

TORAH

According to Jewish tradition, God wrote the words of the Bible on stone tablets and gave them to Moses on Mt. Sinai. Although the original stone tablets have been lost, over the centuries, scribes have copied the words from those tablets by hand onto parchment scrolls, which are kept rolled up and covered inside the Torah Ark in each synagogue.

YOM KIPPUR

This is also called the Day of Atonement, and it is a very special day in the Jewish calendar. Jewish tradition requires that, in order to be forgiven by God on this day, a person must ask for forgiveness from anyone whom they have hurt. On Yom Kippur, all energy is focused on praying and asking forgiveness. At the end of twenty-five hours of prayer comes the final service of the day, the Ne'ilah service.

TRANSLATIONS OF HEBREW NAMES

Ariella: lioness of God
Ba'al Shem Tov: master of a good name
Eliana: God, answer me
Elijah: my God is called Yah [Yah is one of God's names in Hebrew]
Ely [sometimes also spelled Eli]: my God
Ezra: helper
Joshua: may God save
Natan: gift or giver
Rachel: sheep
Samuel: name of God
Shoshana: rose

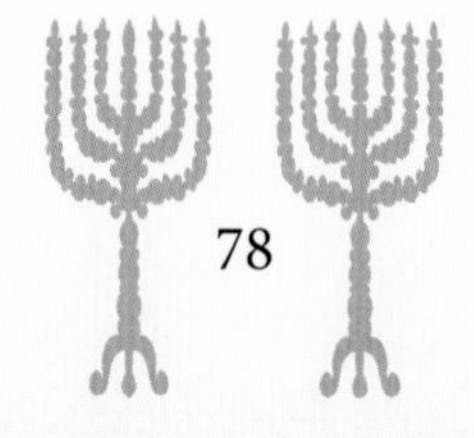

SOURCES

THE POWER OF STORY

This classic Hasidic tale comes from nineteenth-century Eastern Europe. It was first told by Rabbi Yisroel ben Eliezer, a famous rabbi who was also known as the Ba'al Shem Tov, or the "Master of a Good Name." He founded the Hasidic movement, a strand of Judaism that emphasizes spiritual connection with God through prayer, song, story and mysticism.

Buber, Martin. *Tales of the Hasidim: The Later Masters*. New York: Schocken, 1948.

Frankel, Ellen. *The Classic Tales: 4,000 Years of Jewish Lore*. Northvale, NJ: Jason Aronson, 1993.

Schwartz, Howard. *Leaves from the Garden of Eden: One Hundred Classic Jewish Tales*. New York: Oxford University Press, 2009.

Zak, Reuven, ed. *Knesset Israel 13a*. Warsaw, 1866.

ELIJAH'S WISDOM

The prophet Elijah appears in the biblical Book of Kings, but also later becomes a hero of Jewish folklore.

Frankel, Ellen. *The Classic Tales: 4,000 Years of Jewish Lore*. Northvale, NJ: Jason Aronson, 1993.

Rossel, Seymour. *The Essential Jewish Stories*. Jersey City, NJ: KTAV Publishing House, 2011.

THE BOY WHO PRAYED THE ALPHABET

Several versions of this story appear in Hasidic literature. All of them tell of a young boy without formal schooling who prays with such a pure heart that, even though he doesn't know the right words or the proper way to recite them, God hears his prayer anyway.

Frankel, Ellen. *The Classic Tales: 4,000 Years of Jewish Lore*. Northvale, NJ: Jason Aronson, 1993.

Schram, Peninnah. *The Hungry Clothes and Other Jewish Folktales*. New York: Sterling Publishing, 2008.

THE PRINCE WHO THOUGHT HE WAS A ROOSTER

This is a tale by the great Hasidic master Rabbi Nachman of Bratslav, who lived in nineteenth-century Poland. He often taught his students through parables and tales such as this one.

Jungman, Ann. *The Prince who Thought he was a Rooster and Other Jewish Stories.* London: Frances Lincoln, 2007.

Schwartz, Howard. *Leaves from the Garden of Eden: One Hundred Classic Jewish Tales.* New York: Oxford University Press, 2009.

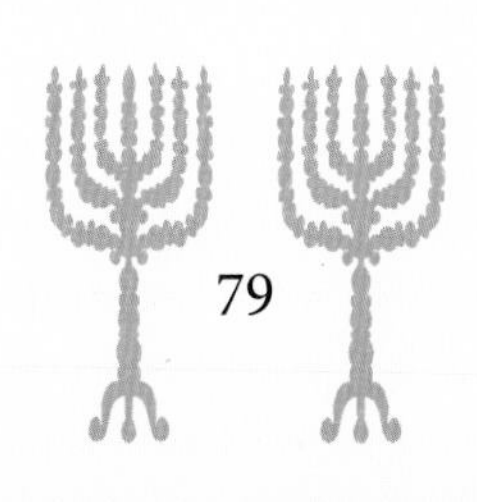

מקורות

CHALLAH IN THE ARK

This story is based on the sixteenth-century tale by Rabbi Isaac Luria (known as "the Ari", which means "the Lion") from *Shivhei ha-Ari* (In Praise of the Ari). Rabbi Luria is considered to be the father of contemporary Kabbalah, or Jewish mysticism.

Rossel, Seymour. *The Essential Jewish Stories*. Jersey City, NJ: KTAV Publishing House, 2011.

Schwartz, Howard, ed. *Gates to the New City: A Treasury of Modern Jewish Tales*. Northvale, NJ: Jason Aronson, 1991.

HEAVEN AND HELL

Versions of this story can be found in several different traditions, including Japanese and Christian folklore. This telling incorporates the Jewish legend of the *lamed-vavnik*s, thirty-six righteous people upon whom the world's existence depends.

Feinstein, Rabbi Edward M. *Capturing the Moon: Classic and Modern Jewish Tales*. Springfield, NJ: Behrman House, 2008.

Outcalt, Todd. *Candles in the Dark: A Treasury of the World's Most Inspiring Parables*. Hoboken, NJ: John Wiley & Sons, 2002.

CLEVER RACHEL

Stories of clever women who solved riddles were popular throughout Eastern Europe. In Jewish tradition, they were often told as examples of the "woman of valor" mentioned in Proverbs 31:10, "*A woman of valor, who can find?*"

Ausubel, Nathan, ed. *A Treasury of Jewish Folklore*. New York: Crown Publishers, 1972.

Cahan, Judah Loeb. *Yiddishe Folksmaisses* (*Yiddish Folk Stories*). New York and Vilna: Ferlag Yiddishe Folklore-Bibliothek, 1931.

Sherman, Josepha. *Rachel the Clever and other Jewish Folktales*. Little Rock, AK: August House, 1993.

THE PERFECT MISTAKE

Originally based on a tale from the eighteenth-century Hasidic teacher, the Maggid of Dubno (also known as Jacob ben Wolf Kranz), this story has become a favorite tale in many religious traditions.

Rossel, Seymour. *The Essential Jewish Stories*. Jersey City, NJ: KTAV Publishing House, 2011.

Schram, Peninnah. *The Hungry Clothes and Other Jewish Folktales*. New York: Sterling Publishing, 2008.

Barefoot Books

step inside a story

At Barefoot Books, we celebrate art and story that opens the hearts and minds of children from all walks of life, focusing on themes that encourage independence of spirit, enthusiasm for learning and respect for the world's diversity. The welfare of our children is dependent on the welfare of the planet, so we source paper from sustainably managed forests and constantly strive to reduce our environmental impact. Playful, beautiful and created to last a lifetime, our products combine the best of the present with the best of the past to educate our children as the caretakers of tomorrow.

www.barefootbooks.com

Rabbi Shoshana Boyd Gelfand

trained at the Jewish Theological Seminary, New York City. She was vice president of the Wexner Heritage Foundation before moving to London to raise her family. She is the author of many books and articles and appears regularly on BBC Radio 2's *Pause for Thought*. Her passion is sharing Jewish wisdom in different and inspiring ways.

Amanda Hall

lives in Cambridge, England and works from a studio called The Shadowhouse at the end of her magical garden. Her glowing illustrations have won her acclaim on both sides of the Atlantic. She exhibits her original illustrations regularly in London at Chris Beetles Gallery. You can visit her website at **www.amandahall-illustration.com**

Debra Messing

is a stage, television and film actress who has won an Emmy award for her starring role in the hit TV series *Will and Grace*. Her film work includes *Along Came Polly* and *The Wedding Date*. She has been awarded a Screen Actors Guild award and a Women in Film Lucy award.